The Night Before Christmas

Clement Clarke Moore

Illustrated by Tom Newsom

Dalmatian Press

The DALMATIAN PRESS name and logo are trademarks of Dalmatian Press, LLC, Franklin, Tennessee 37067.
No part of this book may be reproduced or copied in any form without the written permission of Dalmatian Press.

Printed in China.

'Twas the night before Christmas,
when all through the house
Not a creature was stirring,
not even a mouse.

The stockings were hung
by the chimney with care,
In hopes that St. Nicholas
soon would be there.

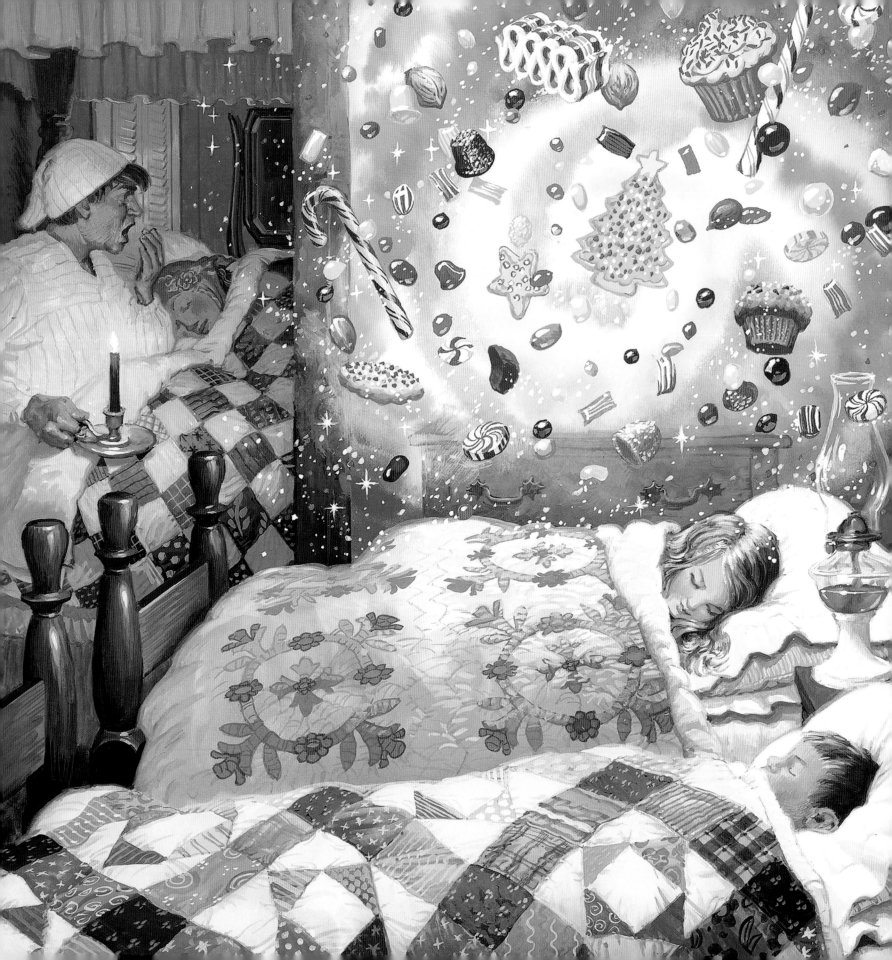

and I in my cap,

Had just settled down

for a long winter's nap,

When out on the lawn
    there arose such a clatter,
I sprang from the bed
    to see what was the matter.

Away to the window
    I flew like a flash,
Tore open the shutters,
    and threw up the sash.

The moon on the breast
    of the new-fallen snow
Gave the luster of midday
    to objects below,

I knew in a moment
it must be St. Nick.

More rapid than eagles
his coursers they came,
And he whistled, and shouted,
and called them by name:

"Now, Dasher! now, Dancer! now, Prancer and Vixen!
On, Comet! on, Cupid! on, Donder and Blitzen!

To the top of the porch!
to the top of the wall!
Now, dash away! dash away!
dash away, all!"

As dry leaves that before
    the wild hurricane fly,
When they meet with an obstacle,
    mount to the sky,

So up to the housetop
    the coursers they flew,
With the sleigh full of toys,
    and St. Nicholas too.

And then, in a twinkling,
    I heard on the roof
The prancing and pawing
    of each little hoof.

As I drew in my head,

  and was turning around,

Down the chimney St. Nicholas

  came with a bound.

He was dressed all in fur,

  from his head to his foot,

And his clothes were all tarnished

  with ashes and soot.

A bundle of toys

  he had flung on his back,

And he looked like a peddler

  just opening his pack.

His eyes—how they twinkled!
his dimples—how merry!
IIis checks were like roses,
his nose like a cherry!

His droll little mouth
was drawn up like a bow,
And the beard of his chin
was as white as the snow.

The stump of a pipe
he held tight in his teeth,
And the smoke it encircled
his head like a wreath.

He had a broad face
   and a little round belly
That shook when he laughed,
   like a bowlful of jelly.

He was chubby and plump—
   a right jolly old elf;
And I laughed when I saw him,
   in spite of myself.

A wink of his eye
   and a twist of his head
Soon gave me to know
   I had nothing to dread.

He spoke not a word,
    but went straight to his work,
And filled all the stockings—
    then turned with a jerk;

And laying his finger
    aside of his nose,
And giving a nod,
    up the chimney he rose!

He sprang to his sleigh,
   to his team gave a whistle,
And away they all flew
   like the down of a thistle.

But I heard him exclaim,
   ere he drove out of sight:

"Happy Christmas to all,
and to all a good night!"